Be My Warlock Tonight

Darklander Lovers series, Book Three

By Renee Field

Be My Warlock Tonight

Darklander Lovers, Volume 3

Renee Field

Published by Renee Field, 2018.

BE MY WARLOCK TONIGHT

First edition. April 2, 2018.

ISBN: 978-1393261612

Written by Renee Field.

Warlocks in Lance's family have been cursed for generations. Revenge pumps in his veins along with his drive to succeed in the human corporate world. During a blind date with his coworker, he discovers she's a witch belonging to the same family who cursed his.

Cindy fought to escape her gray Darklander world to prove herself in the human realm with her business smarts. She dresses down, doesn't use her magic and is a force to be reckoned with.

Ignoring the sizzling passion her demanding warlock lover evokes in her might prove to be the hardest challenge in her life. But enjoying being controlled in the bedroom doesn't mean she has to give up all she's fought for.

Book three in the Darklander Lovers series.

Dedication

This series is dedicated to all the wild women out there looking for a night of fun. Enjoy!

Chapter One

Cindy could not believe her luck. *Damn. Double damn!* Of all the places to meet her blind date of the night it had to be none other than on the tallest building in the city. Forget that heights totally terrified her, but the tallest building...come on, what were the odds? she thought darkly to herself.

I shouldn't have gone to that blasted charity auction. Just think, I could be home in bed now. Alone. That was routine most nights anyway, which was even sadder. However, Cindy was pleased she'd allowed her friends, Nora and Tina, to talk her in to the evening. It had been a pleasantly fun night. In fact, if Cindy didn't know any better she would have thought it had felt almost magical. It also pleased her to know that her hard-earned money went to support a worthwhile cause. The building of the theater's playhouse, next door to the already refurbished cinema, would certainly go a long way to enhancing the downtown block. If she had to fork out a thousand dollars each night over the course of the three-day event it was the least she could do to help the area. Plus as an added bonus she got a date. Something she couldn't seem to get on her own. Another sad point in her life at the moment.

Abruptly Cindy silenced her negative thoughts. She had worked hard for this life and was damn well going to be happy in it.

I can do this. I will do this. Just ignore the fact that this is the tallest building in town and some weirdo had this crazy idea to create a restaurant outside and on the top floor. Sure, why not.

She looked way up at the fifty-plus-story building and fought the urge to flee. Her legs shook, and the belt to her white leather coat was cinched so tight it dug into her waist, but she was determined. If she could negotiate being allowed to live on her own instead of with her family who lived in the Graco-Roman Darklander world, Cindy could conquer her fear of heights and meet her blind date of the night all without the use of magic.

She stepped into the elevator and hit the top floor. When the door opened she awkwardly stepped out.

"May I help you?" The beautiful waitress with unreal long black hair that pooled down past her butt looked at Cindy as if she knew exactly how she felt. *Terrified.*

"I don't think I can do this," she heard herself blurting out.

"Then let me help you." The man's voice rumbled with warmth and familiarity, tickling every nerve ending in her body.

Cindy pivoted and turned. She looked up to find the bluest eyes she'd ever seen. They almost glowed. His pupils were large, aware and there was something mystical...something knowing and telling in those Grecian sea-blue eyes that tightened a knot of dread and excitement in her.

Color was something she never got tired of cataloguing or looking at. Having spent her childhood in the Darklander realm, which existed solely in shades of gray, black and white, Cindy thought Earth was more than she could ever have dreamt about or magically created. She didn't know she had missed anything until she had spied her first red rose.

"And trust me, helping you will feel *ohhh* so good," drawled the man, forcing Cindy back to the moment at hand.

Cindy realized this was her date. He wore the Zorro-like mask to conceal his identity, adding to his allure and making him look sexy as hell in his black formal suit that clung to every chiseled feature on his tall, six-foot-six muscular frame.

Add a sword and he'd look like the perfect Darklander warlock. Rivers of dark jet-black shiny hair fell unfashionably past his shoulders, adding to his mystique. The urge to reach out and run her fingers through his mane flashed hot and bright through her. Then he smiled a sexy, coy grin of knowing. She was instantly hit with his magical magnetism. Goose bumps of lust rose to the occasion and for the first time in her life Cindy was more terrified of the sexual magic this man wielded than her fear of heights.

Still unable to form a coherent word, she let him move closer.

"I will escort you." He claimed her arm, touching her bare skin, and that one fleeting act of intimacy ignited a fire of heat in her pussy that said to hell with the meal, let's just hit the sheets.

Heat rushed to Cindy's cheeks. Her date turned those mystical Grecian-blue eyes to her, grinning devilishly.

"I love your line of thinking."

"And that would be?" Was that *her* throaty voice teasing him? Straightening her spine, Cindy eased more into his frame, purposely brushing her body up against his, needing to feel his reaction.

The tingling zing, as if an electric current passed through her to him, caused his hair to rise in a gentle wave. He simply shook his head and unhooked his arm from hers to bring her hand into his large warm palm.

"Your place or mine?"

"Mine." Cindy didn't hesitate. She had no desire to set one more foot onto the clear see-through floor of Finn's restaurant but she had lots of desire to peel this man layer by layer out of his clothes.

Puff! A second later she squeezed her eyes shut, trying to get orientated. One minute she had been on top of the tallest building in town and then in a blink she was standing inside her house with her blind date looking sexy, dangerous and damn-straight magical.

"Wait a second, you're a magical being?"

"What?" he asked, clearly surprised by her question.

Pissed and angry at herself for not paying better attention to the man she'd picked as her blind date, Cindy sliced him a dirty look.

Placing both hands on her hips, she emphasized her point. "No magical beings."

He sauntered forward, glaring at her. "Are you a witch?"

"Worse. I'm a corporate-climbing bitch with no time for creatures of magic. So...out, out, next time I'll shout." Her sing-song voice resonated enough magical power to zap her blind date back to where he came from.

* * * * *

The silky feel of the black tie Cindy willingly wound around her ankles, tying herself to her own bedposts, ignited a flare of excited goose bumps along her calf muscles.

"I must be crazy." She vaguely felt as if she were missing some important aspect about the night but for the life of her she couldn't think straight.

"No talking."

The mystery man's voice was deep and authoritative. This was a man used to giving orders that others obeyed. Cindy glanced up, catching the heated gaze from his baby-blue eyes. His eyes pierced through the Zorro-like mask, the black cloth serving only to highlight his refined cheekbones, plump full lips and startlingly clear eyes. The mask did its job, keeping her from being able to identify her mystery man. She knew she'd picked him from the charity auction and he was her date for the night, but there were pieces of the puzzle missing. How had she ended up on display for him in her bed? *I must have had more to drink than I thought.*

Without a word he moved to the bed, hooked the silky scarf around her right ankle and appraised her. He trailed a tapered end of the scarf down her thigh to her calf, using it like a finger. Wisps of desire flowed from her leg to her pussy muscles, which clenched anxiously with desire and dread.

"This is what you want."

The man yanked hard on both scarves to ensure she couldn't wiggle her ankles or legs free. Leaning back on her elbows, she chuckled nervously. "Are you reading my mind?"

"You want this."

It was a bold statement coming from a man who was fully clothed while she wasn't. Cindy closed her eyes for a minute, hoping sanity would return.

"Open your eyes," he commanded as he knelt between her spread legs.

"I've changed my mind."

"Maybe, but your body hasn't."

A sexy grin revealed a dimple on his right cheek.

"You're wet. That pussy of yours wants this."

Man, did he ever get that right. Cindy hated how out of control she felt. Her body squirmed with desire while her mind told her this was beyond insane. After all, she didn't know this man. He could do anything to her. *Like tie you to your bed.* Another nervous giggle escaped.

The man walked around to the right side of her bed. Armed with another silk tie, Cindy knew what was coming. Still, her stomach muscles clenched uneasily while her traitorous nipples puckered more. She tried telling herself it was because her bedroom was cool but that was a bold-faced lie.

"Lie down."

She did as instructed. A small moan escaped when he daringly trailed the silk scarf over her wrist, up her arm and down around both breasts. He teased the tips of her nipples with the tapered end, lightly pretending to buff them, causing her body to sway more into the silk. Then a hand clamped on her right wrist. He dragged her arm toward the bedpost to tenderly secure her wrist to the bed with the silk scarf.

There was something warrior-like in the way the man sauntered from the right side of her bed back to the bottom. He stood gazing at her spread-eagle legs.

"I love how your pussy juices are glistening on your curls."

There was a roughness to his voice, a husky timbre that hadn't been there before. The noted reaction of his voice broke through Cindy's rational mind. Knowing he wasn't immune to her allowed the butterflies to flit around in her belly. The idea that he wanted her pleased that thoroughly feminine part of her she kept hidden so well.

Cindy took pride in being the youngest woman to manage one of Xeron's corporations, and she did it all on her own, without using any of her inherent magical abilities she'd purposely disowned. She was the fastest woman, figuratively speaking, to climb up that elusive corporate ladder and it was all due to hard work. She'd gotten there on her business sense, not her looks or her magic, which she'd taken great pains to ignore or play down.

Black or blue knee-length business suits, blonde hair neatly tied up in a bun, and minimal makeup applied every morning. She rarely dated, hardly ever went out to party unless it was work-related, and most assuredly would never have even thought of going on a blind date two weeks ago.

But two things had happened to her recently. First, she'd turned thirty and secondly, her mother had informed her she planned to visit. That wasn't good. Her mother, a member of the Darklander Graco-Roman Witches' Coven, was why Cindy had moved to another world...and sometimes even that distance didn't seem enough.

It had been her friend Tina who'd told her about the charity auction. And voilà, here she was—neatly tied up because she'd insisted all three go, have fun and enjoy a wild, wicked night. Cindy loved her friends but she wasn't stupid enough to let them know she was a witch from another realm. That would get her locked up in an insane asylum within minutes of her confession. Plus they were humans so they could never discover the truth or else the *Vida*—the group of Darklanders who enforced the peace treaty with Earth—would hunt her down and in all likelihood kill her friends. She shivered with that thought. When the man's hand came to rest on her mons, Cindy almost bucked up off the bed.

"I'm not going to ask what you were thinking. But because I know you weren't thinking about what I'm doing to you..."

He paused. Cindy watched him purposely wet his lips.

"I am going to make you pay for that infraction." He lowered his still fully clothed body between her legs.

Like a man knowing exactly what he was looking for, he used his fingers to open her slick pussy lips and took his cursed time doing it. For a moment Cindy felt as if she were being examined but then the soft brush of his breath on her moist opened lips caused her nub to pebble to life.

"Nice and pink for me." He added another soft blow. The erotic tease ignited the flame lying dormant within her.

Oh my god, I'm on the verge of climaxing just from his words.

The man reached up, dragging the arm that wasn't tied to the bedpost down over her belly. When Cindy realized his intent she attempted to pull her hand away. No go. He pulled her hand back down, forcing her fingers to feel her wet juices.

"Keep your lips open for me." He didn't take no for an answer.

"I can't."

"You will. And because you will obey I will treat you."

His tongue plunged deep into her wet opening, the channel of her cunt loving the harsh feel of him. Expertly he pumped his curled tongue over and over into her cunt, giving long licks to the sides of her pussy each and every time he moved it. Gushes of desire slid out her opening, a pink flush of passion surfacing along her achy breasts and chest.

Just when she wanted more, the man moved off her cunt and off the bed.

"What?" she squeaked, mortified. She wanted more. Needed more. She cursed him in her head when the cool air from her bedroom slid over her glistening skin.

"You are not doing what I asked. Now I will ask more of you. I will watch as you pleasure yourself with your fingers."

Another bold statement. He seemed to enjoy pushing her buttons. Something inside her sizzled, leaning toward a light. Cindy knew if she could reach that light she'd remember how all this came to be. Still though, with her body on fire for the feel of his mouth and tongue on her cunt it became a hard push. She wanted him. Wanted the passion her body was beginning to scale the tip of. She desperately yearned for what he would deliver.

If there was one thing Cindy prided herself on it was facing a challenge. Any challenge. This most assuredly was one she had to conquer and overcome. She swallowed her inhibitions and shyness, knowing the reward at the end would be blissful and magically sweet.

Coyly she half-closed her eyes, hoping he wouldn't make her keep them wide open as she slid her free hand down to her mound. Mustering courage, she dipped a finger through the wet opening, feeling how swollen her nether lips had become from his ministrations. Then she plunged a finger deep, her hips instantly moving as she rhythmically fingered her cunt. Masturbating wasn't new to Cindy. Heck, she did the act most nights to unwind in the privacy of her bed or bath. Doing it in front of a complete stranger was edgy and erotic and not something she would have thought she'd do in a million Darklander years.

The soft rustle of clothing being discarded caused her hand and fingers to pause. She opened her eyes wide and gulped.

"This is your treat for obeying." He unzipped his black dress pants. His crisp white dress shirt already lay on the floor.

Cindy's eyes widened appreciably. His chest was muscular and tanned. His skin coloring was a dark shade of cinnamon, and she knew inherently it was natural. With his jet-black curly hair, tanned looks and blue eyes she guessed he had to be at least part Greek. Human men who were inherently Greek had always reminded her of the men from her Darklander Graco-Roman village. When he stepped out of his slacks, revealing he went commando, she guessed he must be fully Greek.

His impressive erection stood pulsing and proud before him.

Oh yeah, that's something to be proud of. Cindy gulped with need as a heated pool of desire caused her pussy muscles to clench with greed while her mouth went dry.

With ease she watched him wrap a hand around his impressive cock, pumping it slowly.

"I'm leveling the playing field."

Cindy could only nod. Speaking meant coherent thought and all she could say was "Wow".

"You did good with your hand, but I'm going to do better," he announced. A moment later he sauntered buck-naked to the other side of the bed, took her free arm in his hand and used the last silk tie to secure her firmly to the bed.

Then he leaned over her, the muscles in his abdomen flexed while his erection inched toward her right nipple. *Being fully secured to the bed does not level the playing field.* Cindy wet her lips in anticipation, her eyes savoring every angle of his impressive cock. Circumcised, the smooth head gleamed almost purple with desire. The tight veins in his impressive member stood out starkly...begging for her lips and hands.

He knelt on her queen-sized bed, took his erection once again in his hand and tapped the round, wet end of his shaft to her budded nipple.

A shiver of desire rippled through Cindy's body. Her hips and chest arched to meet his cock. *Who knew having a man's cock slap your nipples could be such a turn-on?* Well, others might know that but not Cindy. She was sexually inexperienced. She didn't normally indulge in her fantasies, except for this one time. Cindy whimpered when he repeated the action, sliding his cock over the achy tip of her other nipple, wetting it with his own cum. She felt branded. And loved it.

"My cum is going to be all over you. In your mouth, on your breasts, on your stomach and in that cunt of yours. We've got a long night ahead of us and I plan to guarantee you complete satisfaction."

Cindy's entire body throbbed as pulses of desire from his erotic words caused her to pant with need. His promise of delivery almost caused her to climax. She squeezed her eyes shut, wishing she could clamp her legs together to help ease the ache in her pussy, but that was no longer possible. Her arms and legs instinctively bucked against the silk scarves, but they did their job as expertly as her mystery date.

"Now where was I? Yes, that's right. Open your mouth for me. Wide."

Another demand. A blunt one at that and she bristled. When she didn't comply immediately the man tweaked both her nipples hard. She gritted her teeth as her body warred again with the bolts of pain and pleasure spiking through her.

"I said open wide. I'm going to stuff my cock into that lovely mouth of yours."

This time she did as instructed.

"Good girl." A moment later he moved his entire body over hers to position his cock and large balls directly in her face. Using his hand, he pushed the tip of his large shaft in her mouth.

Cindy wasn't sure she'd be able to do this, but now she had no choice. The girth of his shaft was wide but thankfully he seemed to know she needed time to adjust to having her mouth stuffed with his member.

"That's it. A bit more."

She gulped, fighting past her gag reflex. It was a heady moment for her. She'd only done one other blowjob in her life and that felt nothing like this. That had been more like a thirty-second cock-in-your-mouth experience. This man, slow and patient, let her body and mouth get used to the feel of his large cock. Tenderly, he withdrew. She licked her tongue along the hard vein and was pleased when he answered her explorations with a moan.

Cindy wanted his cock back in her mouth. Thankfully he obliged, sliding it back as she tilted her head up to meet him. She watched him cup his balls, the soft sac teasing her lips. This time when he removed his cock from her mouth, she darted her tongue over the slick opening at the top. Before he plunged it back into her mouth she spoke.

"Can I lick your balls?"

The muscles in his gut flexed. This time he was speechless. He nodded, and then because her hands were tied he had to use his hands to bring the large weights to her mouth. She darted her tongue out, licking the wrinkly sac, loving the rubbery feel of it. Opening her mouth wider, she felt a thrill of discovery settle in her when he allowed her to pull one of his testicles deep inside the recesses of her mouth. A guttural groan tore from him, which encouraged her ministrations. Using her mouth and tongue, she teased his testicle and repeated the action with his second ball when he pushed that deep inside her mouth.

"Enough."

Cindy knew his harsh tone masked his desire. She knew all about that.

Without a word, his body skimmed down hers. He trailed a tender line of kisses from her wrists, arms, and the underside of her belly straight to her still-sensitive cunt. Then he plunged a finger deep inside her. A magical jolt of desire shot through her.

"I'm going to finger-fuck you first and you're going to watch."

Again his wicked words teased the naughty woman she let out to play tonight.

She felt him twist his hand, his finger pumping toward her stomach as he patted an ultrasensitive spot deep inside her cunt. She squirmed, not used to the feeling.

"Relax. You will enjoy."

He was masterfully sure of himself. She willed her body to relax and after another minute her cunt muscles responded to his drumbeat on the squishy pad he pressed deep inside her. It was a spot she'd only read about. The man...the mystery man...had found her G-spot, something she'd tried countless times to discover herself with no luck.

"I want your pussy juices all over my hand so I can lick every speck of your cum off my fingers."

He picked up his repeated drumming on her G-spot. The pressure built within her body and a momentary panic gripped her.

"Trust me, it will feel magical," he said, using his other hand to tweak her pebbled nub. The action caused her body to heave off the bed. Still he didn't relent. His finger padded over and over again on her ultrasensitive spot deep within her cunt and then the most magical thing happened. She came. One long stream of hot liquid cum jetted out of her pussy.

"That's it, baby. So good." His mouth lapped up every intimate speck of cum that seeped from her. Reverently and tenderly she felt his mouth kissing her swollen nether lips, moving to the insides of her thighs as his tongue lapped up her juices. Her body became limp. More sexually satisfied than she'd ever been in her life, Cindy knew the night had only started. She grinned with that thought while closing her eyes in ecstasy.

"Your cum tastes so good. Like sweet white Graco wine. Now I'm going to change your position."

Vaguely she wondered if she heard him wrong. She could have sworn he said Graco wine. Thinking he really meant Greek wine, she sleepily watched him untie all the silk scarves. He moved her to the edge of the bed and retied her arms, forcing them behind her back. Now he had her attention. She was fully awake. A zing of electric chemistry, of knowing what he was going to do to her, caused her mouth to salivate.

"My turn."

With deliberate slowness he pushed the pulsing, thick ridge of his cock deep inside her mouth.

"Take it, baby. You can and you will."

Chapter Two

Lance couldn't stop smiling. His ultimate fantasy had come true. Who knew being talked by his sister into participating in the ridiculous Darklander auction would be so much fun? In full warlock mode he had sauntered with pride up and down the theater's stage, hands on his hips, posing, letting them get a good look at his body clad in the form-fitting black tuxedo.

The oohs and ahhs of the women had burned through him, leaving him edgy and horny. Then when he finished and his sister had handed him the envelope with the yellow daisy he had to give to his blind date, he saw stars for the first time. Lance had seen his sister give the matching daisy to Cindy Frost, his coworker and the woman he'd asked out twice only to be crushed double-time by her. Cindy was tonight's blind date.

Every man at Xeron thought of her as frigid and dull and all business. But not Lance. He knew deep down in his gut that Cindy was anything but what her last name implied. Driven, successful, sexy and wild. While the first two attributes were easy to see because that's how she wanted people to view her, Lance knew the other two traits were ones she possessed and longed for. He'd say it was what his warlock heart and soul could discern if anyone asked him, which of course happened. He'd told Hank and Mitch, his two buddies, and they'd laughed their collective asses off. They had laughed even harder when he told them he'd mustered the courage to ask her out only to be knocked down hard, twice.

If he really wanted to he could have used his magic at night to seduce her, but that idea had never sat well with Lance. Until tonight.

Hearing the word "magic" fly out of Cindy's mouth and then feeling every powerful wisp of her Darklander powers, which had sent him reeling back to that blasted stage where he'd been strutting his stuff, had unleashed something dangerous and wild within him.

To Darklander g'ulot *with the blasted rules.* Immediately Lance flashed back into her townhouse, slightly amazed he'd been able to do so with ease. For a powerful witch she didn't use any protectorates. No warding spells to guard her dwelling, no annoying sugar spilled around the windows to trick his mind into forgetting his mission and thankfully no cats to hiss their displeasure at him. Lance snorted. He usually got enough hissing from Hank, not that he'd ever let on to his werecat buddy that he hated felines of all kinds. Hank was a different sort—more beast than cat.

Lance's mission was to get to Cindy. So he'd landed in her house and before she could open her mouth he'd rearranged her memories, taken her witch powers from her and ensured when he left she'd only vaguely remember him. His warlock nature couldn't resist making her think she had been his blind date and that she wanted him to fulfill her ultimate fantasy. *It's payback time, baby.*

Lance had only tonight, because come dawn all his warlock powers vanished thanks to the stupidity of one of his ancient relatives, a Papadopoulos warlock who had dared to wrong one cantankerous witch. Never cross a witch. Especially not a Stephanopoulos witch. Not only could they burn you with a simple chant, causing your body to combust, but they were so mean they'd make sure your entire family went up in smoke with you. *Yeah, the Stephanopoulos witches were true bitches.* Hank silently snickered with his own thoughts.

Now who has the last laugh? Lance watched his rigid cock slide sweetly into Cindy's welcoming mouth. His body vibrated and hummed with magical energy, swamping his senses. Lance swayed on the balls of his feet as Cindy quickly learned what his cock enjoyed, which was everything her perky mouth and tongue were currently doing to his member. He especially loved it when he dragged his shaft out of her mouth so she could slide her tongue along the thick tender vein on the underside. Then he plunged it back down her throat, pushing her limits.

Just as I thought, a wild side. He fought the ragged groan that tore from him when she deep throated almost all of him.

His hand fisted around her silky long blonde hair. Surprising her by popping unannounced into her house, Lance had his first glimpse of her enticing honey-wheat-colored hair and his breath had hitched. Having only seen her hair in its usual no-nonsense tight bun, he'd had no idea of its length. Her hair came to rest at her tailbone and it was every man's fantasy—blonde, long and unbelievably silky smooth. Lance tightened his hold on the strands fisted in his hands. He longed to bring the ends of her hair up to his nose for a good whiff of that jasmine-scented shampoo of hers that had always driven him nuts.

A small whimper from Cindy drew his attention to what he asked of her. Lance knew his cock was large and there was no way she'd be able to take the entire length of his member down her throat. So at first he'd been slow and tender, letting her get used to the feel of his large shaft invading her mouth and throat. For a moment he wondered how it would feel to have her hand fisted around the base of his cock, pumping him for all he was worth while he worked her mouth. He thought about untying her hands but then thought better of it.

There was a part deep within Cindy that wanted to be tied up. Taken and used so she could pretend she had no control over what was happening to her and Lance was only too happy to oblige. He was glad he used his magic to discern her innermost thoughts.

"I'm going to come in your mouth. You're going to swallow all of me as I pump it down your throat."

He blinked, watching the effect of his words. Her light blue eyes rounded up in anticipation. She curled her tongue, swiveling it around the large column of his cock. Picking up the pace, Lance let himself get lost in the rhythm his cock thoroughly enjoyed. He felt his balls bunch tight, his cum seconds away from exploding from the wet slit at the opening of his shaft. For one second he thought about pulling out but then thought better of it. Shoving his shaft down her throat, Lance pushed it past her gag point, knowing she used willpower to keep it down. He came in a hot jet and loved how Cindy's throat muscles swallowed him whole. Slowly he pulled his still semi-rigid cock out of her mouth, thrilled she took the time to lick him clean.

Lance couldn't stop himself. He needed to feel those lips of hers. Leaning down, he cupped her head in his large hands and kissed her on the mouth. There was a moment's hesitation on her part, as if her true self tried to reassert itself, forcing Lance to quickly double his spell, to ensure the binding kept. Then blessedly she opened up. Lance plundered that plump red mouth he'd been dreaming about for months with a thank-you kiss, tasting his own cum on her tongue and lips, causing his body to immediately respond for more.

This was the last thing Lance had expected tonight.

The minute Lance had stepped up to Cindy, feeling her nervous energy as she attempted to talk herself into walking into Finn's restaurant located on the tallest office building in town, his cock had bucked to attention. When he read her thoughts that said she wanted to peel him layer from layer out of his clothes, pure, unbridled lust had seized his magical powers. Flashing them both to her house had been easy. After all, he knew where she lived because the first time he'd asked her out had been while driving her home after an afternoon business party where she'd had one too many. Thankfully, he was pretty certain she'd been too drunk to remember laughing at him and saying no way when he'd asked her out. Pride hurt, he'd shut his mouth but gallantly escorted her to her door, leaving once she was safely inside and the door re-locked.

The second time he'd mustered his stupid courage to ask her out had been after getting his first promotion. On par with her, they were each managers of one of Xeron's divisions. Each of them was also determined to secure the upcoming CEO position once their current boss retired in a few months. Nothing like proving yourself in the human, corporate world to show your fellow warlocks not only did you have balls where it counted but you were a killer in the business realm. Business was something Papadopoulos warlocks were especially good at.

They had both been in the elevator when it had gone out of commission. Still reeling and feeling like a warlock making his first kill, Lance had leaned over toward Cindy, noting she'd looked slightly pissed at being stuck in the elevator with him. He'd stated he had been looking for the perfect opportunity to ask her out to dinner. She'd told him none too politely she didn't think that was a wise move. Thankfully, the elevator had resumed its downward journey to avoid the embarrassing quiet that had settled in the space.

Now here he was kissing the life out of her after she'd given him the best blowjob of his life. Just knowing his cum was inside her and that this was only part of her fantasy fired his cock back to life.

If there was one thing Cindy was it was detailed. Using magic, Lance had read her mind. Her fantasy was every man's wet dream. She wanted a man who controlled her. A man who made her do things she might not normally want. A man who wouldn't take no for an answer. While he wasn't a man, Lance certainly was the perfect warlock for the job.

Breaking the kiss, he pushed her down on the bed. With her arms tied behind her back, she was slightly helpless, something she didn't normally allow. Once again Lance admired her body. Tall at an even five-foot-eight with her blonde hair cascading down her back, light blue eyes, lithe frame and bountiful breasts, she was the complete picture of Avera, the Darklander Graco-Roman Goddess of Love and War. When one factored in Cindy's smarts and her killer attitude when it came to business, Lance knew this woman was more a warrior than a lover because that was what she'd convinced herself of. The fact she was a witch had thrown him for a loop. Lance wasn't stupid. He knew there were human witches but he'd only ever caught wisps of their power at night.

In the year they worked for the same company not once had he caught a hint of Cindy's witch powers. *Mind you in the day I'm basically a pathetic human.* The knowledge of that ripped through Lance.

Knowing Cindy was a witch and she possessed a wild side was a bonus. He was the perfect Darklander warlock for her and was bound and determined to show her that both traits co-existed within her.

Lance shook his head. *When did I start down that poetic road?* Startled with his own references, Lance knew Cindy Frost had to be your typical human witch. She looked like his Goddess but he'd listened to her butcher his own last name, Papadopoulos, enough times to know she wasn't from his world. She probably didn't have a speck of human Greek heritage running through her veins, because for the life of her she couldn't pronounce his last name without stumbling.

"Turn over," he demanded.

More than anything Lance wanted to see Cindy's bare ass. She always wore tight business skirts, either black or blue in color, and while they looked somewhat demure coming to rest at her knees, he'd eyed her rump every time she'd bent over. It had provided him with a remarkable view. *But this view will be much better.* Lance couldn't wait to eye the plump curves of her ass cheeks.

He watched her awkwardly move her body from her back to her belly. It wasn't easy to do with her wrists tied together but as much as he wanted to help he couldn't as it would ruin her fantasy.

"On your knees."

"What?"

He gave a hard smack to her ass. "I didn't tell you to speak."

Fire sparked to life in her blue eyes when she turned her head to observe him. He gave her the span of ten seconds, knowing she fought with herself. Wanting it but worried she might be getting in over her head, which of course she was. Lance grinned. Her seconds were up.

"Knees. Now," he demanded, moving his body.

This time she complied. She balanced her weight on her knees by spreading her legs because her wrists were tied together. Still though Lance knew the position was awkward for her.

"What are you going to do?"

Lance noted her tone had become breathless and erratic. He untied the silky scarves without speaking. She immediately balanced herself on the palms of her hands on the bed.

Good girl. "Obey and enjoy." He followed his words with a second hard smack on her ass. Lance took great delight in seeing the red outline from his hand on her cheek. He loved her gasp of feigned outrage. Behind that outrage was passion and he planned to bring her over her limit, so much so she'd be sore tomorrow. Sexually satisfied, tired and happy, he wanted to imprint every part of her lush body to ensure she didn't forget him.

He wanted to ram his cock into her pussy, over and over again. After all that had been his fantasy the minute he'd met the cool, level-headed woman who had made it clear to him that she thought she was better than him. Well, after tonight she could think that all she wanted. He was her fantasy lover for one night and if that was all he got from Cindy then he wasn't about to waste one minute of it.

"I'm going to fuck you hard because you didn't obey me." *And because you turned me down twice and pissed off one mighty warlock!*

Chapter Three

Cindy's body was sore in places she'd never expected. Her butt cheeks were still slightly red and splotchy from the spankings her mystery lover had given her last night, hence why she sat on one cheek. And her nipples. Who knew the light feel of her crisp white-collared shirt would actually make them ache? Her pussy still felt swollen and even though she'd taken a hot shower, she felt as if her body remembered the feel of his skillful hands and mouth on her skin when she closed her eyes. Talk about romantic. Immediately, she wanted to smack her head.

There really was nothing remotely romantic about last night. She did remember going to the auction and placing bids on a man but for the universe she couldn't seem to figure out how she'd ended up in bed with her blind date. Cindy rubbed her temples in a small repeating pattern, hoping to unlock the fuzziness in her brain, which screamed at her she was missing something important.

She'd had four hours of hot, erotic, mind-blowing sex with a complete stranger. With a man she didn't even know. She did know he was masterful and considerate and had taken the time always to put a condom on. He'd pushed her buttons but she'd loved it and that had surprised her. While nameless, Cindy knew in her heart she'd never forget him.

For the first time in years she thought her magic would come in handy. *I could cast a spell, bind my mystery lover to me but then it wouldn't be real, would it?* Cindy drew a sharp breath in, rearranged her business folders and realized the enormity of her wayward thoughts. *Magic!* That temptation to use what coursed through her veins and mind made her nervous. She had survived this long with the charade of being human so Cindy wasn't about to let one man take all she had gained—her independence, her freedom and choice of lifestyle—away from her. Using business smarts, she'd get what she wanted.

If Cindy used magic three times in one moon-cycle she'd be forced back home to the Darklander realm. Worse, she'd end up having to work for the Graco-Roman Witches' Coven for the rest of her life. She blinked hard. *Not in this lifetime.*

Using her brain power and business sense, she had worked hard to be allowed to go to a human university, get a job and work her way to the top. A thrill of potentially getting what she wanted felt like a caffeine jolt to her system. Before she could thoroughly plan her maneuvering her office phone rang. It was Nora.

"Spill."

Nora's soft purring voice, slightly anxious, teased Cindy. Knowing Nora as Cindy had since their university days, the poor woman had probably been up all night worried sick about Cindy giving in to the wild side.

"No way."

"Oh. My. God! You actually did it. You went to Finn's and let the wild side out. I can hear it in your voice."

"Maybe." Cindy attempted to swivel her chair around but that proved hard to accomplish when only one butt cheek firmly rested on the leather seat. Pulling on an earring, Cindy had no idea what Nora was talking about.

"Why would I go to Finn's?" asked Cindy.

An audible pause filled the line. "Cindy, you were to meet your blind date at Finn's Restaurant."

Cindy gave a choked chuckle. "I was?" Clearly perplexed, Cindy had no recollection of that. She vividly remembered enjoying the night with her friends at the auction, but no way she'd set foot inside Finn's Restaurant, located on the outside of the tallest building in the city. Without the use of her magic, heights terrified her.

"Details, baby, details," demanded Nora.

Normally, Cindy loved to spill all the beans to her best friend, Nora or even to Tina, but this time she didn't want to. Until she had all the answers and felt more like herself she planned to keep her worries to herself. *What's real and what's not?*

Switching topics, she asked, "So how was your date?"

"Great."

That one word said it all.

"Oh Nora, I'm so sorry."

"Don't be. I'm not. I'll get my satisfaction so don't worry about me. Look, I've got to run. And, Cindy Stephanopoulos Frost, I am your best friend. I will get the details out of you. It's only a matter of time," Nora stated in the best mother-hen voice she could muster.

Trust Nora to resort to saying my full name to get my attention. Credits, girl. Cindy gave two to Nora for that one. No one, except of course obviously Nora, knew Cindy Frost, a.k.a. Cindy Stephanopoulos Frost, had a name that sounded remotely Greek in the human world. Cindy knew if her friend ever found out she wasn't from this world, both their lives would never be the same again.

Cindy had inadvertently tossed out her so-called middle name one night during a drunken stupor. Thankfully she hadn't said anything about witches and the Darklander realm. When Cindy's mother had married a non-Graco-Roman warlock she'd taken his last name in marriage. When her father had left them when she was two, her mother had cast him out of their village for good and hadn't bothered to change Cindy's last name. If there was one thing Cindy had learned early in her business career it was that having an ethnic name was a stumbling block for those human white males who lined that elusive ivory tower.

"Okay, here's the deal. After your date tonight I will spill the beans. Are you still meeting us later at the theater for the second night of bidding?" asked Cindy.

"Of course. Nothing in this world could make me miss it," chuckled Nora, her voice a husky purr.

"What's come over you? Your voice sounds strange," said Cindy.

Nora cleared her throat. "Nothing's wrong with my voice and I'll share my secret when you tell me yours." She giggled.

Cindy laughed with her. It was impossible not to. "Okay, be mysterious. I'll see you later tonight."

"Deal," chimed Nora. "Gotta run."

Yeah, I bet. Cindy knew exactly what Nora meant about running. She planned to let her fingers run across her cell phone so she could call Tina and break the news to her that Cindy had *done it.*

As she hung up her phone, a daring plan popped into Cindy's head. She opened her email and fired off a terse note before talking herself out of it. *Oh yeah, baby, he'll be pissed off and demand a second chance.* Smiling smugly to herself, Cindy was thrilled and terrified at the same time with what she had set in motion—demanding a refund.

Firing off an email to Madam Sasha, the manager and coordinator of the blind date charity auction, without thought was uncharacteristic for Cindy. Last night Sasha had given Cindy her business card. Now Cindy demanded her own satisfaction, stating the man she'd paid a thousand dollars for wasn't worth it. Inwardly, she laughed.

My ass, she thought, quite literally, knowing Mr. Unsatisfactory would demand a second chance to ensure she was fully satisfied with his services. Deciding it was time to get her morning coffee now that'd she'd executed her first order of the day, Cindy practically hummed stepping into the elevator thinking, *Baby come to momma.*

"You're happy this morning. Must have been a good night."

Lost in her own daydreams, Cindy blinked to clear her thoughts and forced herself to stop humming. For a second she could have sworn she'd heard her mystery lover's voice here in the elevator with her. Weird.

Turning her head to the right, she noticed Lance Papadopoulos leaning with his back against the elevator wall. The light in the elevator was dim at the best of times and with his neat black business suit and dark navy dress shirt she hadn't been aware of him.

"So was it a good night?"

"What?" she asked, clearing her throat.

He leaned a little closer to her, and for one second Cindy thought she caught a whiff of sweet, hot melting candy. Pursing her lips, she dismissed that, noting the hint of malice in Lance's voice. *Ridiculous. It's just Lance.* The hotshot Greek human who would soon be eating dust when she became the next CEO. The same hunk who had every woman in all the departments panting with lust. But not her. Cindy made it a rule not to date coworkers. Even coworkers as charming and dangerously good-looking as Lance. Plus, dating to her mother meant marriage. Either a wedding or be turned into a toad. *So not funny.*

"Did you have a good night last night?"

"The usual." She pressed the bottom button. For a moment she wondered why the button hadn't been already pressed because it appeared as if Lance had been in the elevator before her. *Surely he wasn't in here waiting to talk to me.* Cindy cast another glance Lance's way.

His dark hands trailed through the thick black wavy hair on his head and for a moment she caught a glimpse of her mystery lover. She physically shook her head. *It's just because he's Greek and the guy last night was Greek. That's it.* Still though, it took a lot of willpower on Cindy's part not to thoroughly check out Lance as he leaned casually against the elevator wall all but staring at her. *Now if he'd do a slow strip-tease, then I'd know for sure it wasn't him.* She chuckled.

"Something funny?" he snarled.

"What?"

"You're chuckling. Am I missing some private joke here?"

Cindy smoothed her now sweaty palms over her blue skirt. "No. I was just remembering something."

"Really, I bet it's not what you think it is," he mumbled.

"What?" She turned and looked at him, thinking this had to be the most confusing conversation she'd had in a long time. His blue eyes were all but shooting daggers at her. "Someone got up on the wrong side of the bed this morning," she teased.

"Not the wrong side of the bed...wrong bed," he stated flatly, staring at her in earnest.

A shiver of fear spiked through Cindy, causing goose bumps of warning to zing across her skin. Thankfully she was saved by the bell. "TMI, Lance. Grab a coffee, you'll feel better. That always works for me." With a spring in her step Cindy stepped out of the elevator and into the lobby with a smile.

"Oh I'll be grabbing something later, don't you worry...you'll be the first to know."

With that cryptic remark Lance marched past her, oblivious to the sighs and glances from all the women in the lobby who were ogling his muscular body that the polished business suit showcased with ease. Her eyes got caught on his ass, clearly outlined in his black suit pants as he marched through the corridor, looking madder than an enraged bull.

Good thing he isn't a magical being because adding his handsome good looks and magic together would make for one volcanic recipe.

Cindy smiled. There was nothing remotely magical about Lance. Giving up her own magical powers, much to her mother's horror and forever consternation, didn't mean she couldn't smell a magical being. The few times she had run across Darklander beings laced with magic she'd caught that sweet, hot, melting candy scent and wisely backed away. He reeked of hot, intent male and that was enough.

Cindy's heart started to palpitate when she realized the seriousness of what she'd set into motion. She'd basically told Sasha her date didn't perform. She'd called into question his masculinity. Cindy gulped and ran for the coffee house across the street, not caring in her haste she wove in and out of traffic.

The truth of what she'd now set in motion spun in her mind faster than a crazed broomstick. A deadly magical message flashed through her mind telling her she was in a deep, boiling cauldron trouble.

* * * * *

Lance swiveled his office chair around to watch Cindy walk past him wearing one of her no-nonsense blue business suits. Like a spy he took great satisfaction as she plopped her ass down in her chair. She grimaced and he knew why. He'd fucked her long and thoroughly, spanking her round cheeks even harder, and she'd come twice for him—once while she'd been on her knees, ass in the air with his cock in her cunt, and the other time when he'd tied her face-down, stuffed a pillow under her hips to leverage her butt and smacked her cheeks, feigning outrage that she'd come when he'd told her not to.

She had thrashed around and pretended not to enjoy his punishment but the minute he plunged a finger into her dripping wet core her pussy muscles had clenched around it like a spandex glove and she'd come hard, her body spiraling with passion. Slightly dazed, he then flipped her over, untied the silk scarf from her wrists and donned another condom so he could quickly fill her cunt with his achy cock. And then he'd taken his time with her. They played out the fucking, taking delight in each other's body, each other's desires. By the time Lance had left around four in the morning his cock had hurt and his balls had ached. He'd come four times in four hours. A record for him.

The phone buzzed in his right pants pocket, interrupting his thoughts, a good thing judging by the reaction of his cock. He turned his chair so his back was to his office door, forcing his eyes away from Cindy, whose office was directly opposite his.

"Have you checked your email?"

Mitch's voice cut through him. His Darklander vampire buddy who worked the night shift as a human police officer sounded annoyed. It was the perfect job for his pissed-off-with-life buddy. Lance was pleased the Mistress of the Darklander Council had granted Mitch a stay in the human world. Until fairly recently the Darklander realm had been in a state of beastly clan wars with fairies, drákon, vampires, the sidhe, warlocks and witches fighting each other. A peace of sorts had finally emerged thanks to the Mistress. With peace also came prosperity and

Lance, besides being a mighty warlock, was a mighty fast learner in the business-corporate world. Mergers and acquisitions thrilled him as much as facing a crazed drákon.

"What?" asked Lance.

"Email. Check it."

Taking orders didn't sit well with Lance. Normally he'd tell anyone else to fuck off but not Mitch. Besides being a great cop, Mitch was a killer vampire and the best buddy a warlock could have. When he gave an order you responded because Mitch was the type of vampire who didn't put up with any shit, but he was also the type of guy who'd take out your enemy for you without a second thought.

Lance clicked his email icon, watching as a dozen new messages popped up on the screen. His eyes flared when the red flagged email popped up. Immediately he opened it, still keeping his cell phone open with his other hand. Twice Lance read the email. It didn't make any sense to him.

"Fuck, Mitch, what does that mean?"

"It means your sister is one mad witch. She says the client emailed her stating you didn't deliver your end of the blind date agreement. I'm so glad I'm not you. I have my own problems."

The dead sarcasm wasn't lost on Lance.

Didn't deliver? Try like four fucking times! Lance knew his buddy would view that disclosure as TMI.

"Your sister said not to bother showing up for the second night of the auction. She's really mad at you. I don't know what you did to that date of yours but you must have pissed her off completely."

Hot searing outrage flashed through Lance. *Not bloody likely.* "Who's taking my number?"

"Some warlock named Marcus."

Lance didn't say anything else. He clicked his cell phone closed, deleted the email and stormed out of his office. Marcus. There was no way Marcus, his cousin, was going to take his number and strut his stuff tonight. *Didn't deliver. Cindy, you are so going to wish you didn't say that.* Because not even if the Darklander *g'ulot* froze over would Lance let Marcus anywhere near his woman...witch, *whatever.*

Lance looked at his watch. Nine hours until the sun set and then he'd have all his warlock powers and little witchy Cindy Frost had better look out. One Darklander warlock was coming for her and he wasn't smiling.

* * * * *

Lance slid into the diner's leather seat, ordered a coffee from a passing waitress and listened to the conversation taking place between Mitch and Hank.

"I knew we should have said no to your sister, Lance." Mitch's voice was gruff and dead serious.

"When was the last time you tried to say no to Sasha?"

Lance halfheartedly paid attention to both Mitch's and Hank's tales. It sounded as if they were all in deep shit. Being in the human realm was hard enough, but with what had happened to them last night Lance's senses told him things were about to get worse.

"I can top you guys. My date of the evening doesn't even remember me. Thank the universe. She was a bloody witch."

"I thought you liked witches," said Hank, his werecat buddy.

"I normally do. She, however, obviously hates warlocks. The minute she realized I was magical she cast me back to that theater quicker than you could wink, which pissed me off."

"So naturally you went all macho-warlock on her and used a spell to ensure she wouldn't remember you." Sarcasm dripped from Mitch's voice.

"Of course. By the way did I mention the witch is none other than my coworker Cindy Frost?"

"No shit," exclaimed both Hank and Mitch.

"Yup."

31

"Wait a sec. Isn't this the same woman you asked out and were turned down cold? And the same person who fired off that email to your sister saying you didn't deliver?" Mitch gave an evil chuckle. Hank grinned, flashing those pearly whites that could dazzle a woman.

"Shut up." Lance desperately wanted to give both his buddies a good zap in the ass but knew that would make things worse.

"Man, that's one pissed, angry woman," teased Hank.

"She's not a woman. She's a witch. Did you miss that part of the sentence, you illiterate feline?" growled Lance. He flicked his finger and a hot cheeseburger appeared in front of him. He made sure his magic blocked the patrons from seeing his parlor tricks and then wolfed down the burger before the waitress noticed.

Hank snarled. His hair almost stood on end. "Who are you calling illiterate? 'Cause I know it ain't me. I've got a doctor in front of my name and all you've got is...nothing. And I've told you a hundred times, don't use magic in public."

"So what's your problem anyway, Lance?" asked Mitch.

Lance knew it was a diversionary tactic, which was probably for the best.

"Good thing she doesn't remember me. I cast a forget-me spell on her and worked my own magic in the sheets, if you get my meaning," said Lance, grinning.

"At least the sun had set and you were able to do that," said Hank, patting down his fly-away hair.

"How come you didn't know she was a witch before?" asked Mitch.

Lance glared at his friend. "Duh, because it was day. Ain't got no power in the day, man, kind of like you."

"Yeah, don't remind me," said Mitch, pushing around the food on his plate to make it look as if he'd eaten. "We're all having problems with our women and tonight we have to strut our stuff again. We can't let Sasha down, she's counting on us."

"Don't I know that," said Lance, grimacing. "However there is no way I'm about to let my cousin on that stage. I worked out things with my sister and she's agreed that I can have one more chance and trust me, after tonight Cindy had better look out."

"Why does my gut tell me you've got something dark and sinister planned for that witch?" added Hank, in between bites of his rare cheeseburger.

Lance took a sip of his coffee and grinned. "Dark and sinister sounds about right. After all, my date didn't call in to tell *your* sister that you didn't deliver in the sheets. Yeah, that's what I thought. Nope. Well, trust me, after tonight, Cindy will be begging for my touch and my sister won't be laughing her ass off at me anymore."

Mitch and Hank chuckled but Lance knew the only one laughing after tonight would be him. Sweet magical satisfaction, he couldn't wait to get started.

Sobering, Mitch added, "Trust me, all our problems are serious. Here's what I propose. We strut our stuff, let the women bid on us and then fuck them senseless."

Lance nodded his agreement. His erection pressed tight to his pants as he envisioned fucking Cindy over and over again until his balls ached and she could say his name fluently and slowly, like a lover's caress.

Chapter Four

Sitting through night two of the charity auction was absolute torture for Cindy. The urge to flee and leave her friends soared through her. She was especially thankful she had left her magical broomstick at home in the Darklander realm.

She had watched her blind date from the previous night perform onstage. Slowly he had shed his clothing for the crowd of encouraging women. Not being able to take it any longer, Cindy had bolted out of the theater's hall into the side alley, not caring she left her friends in the lurch. She couldn't take another minute of watching her mystery date strip for other women.

"Going somewhere?"

Cindy didn't need magic to know that voice belonged to none other than her mystery man. In an instant she wished she had brought her broomstick with her. Finally in the human realm she'd be able to put her stick to good use, all without using magic because her plan was simple—she'd use the blunt end to smash him senseless.

She couldn't believe she'd willingly sat through his performance. The urge to cast a spell and whisk him away from the crowd had throbbed through her. Cindy shivered. She felt his magnetic pull as it stimulated every part of her, especially her pussy which felt drenched with want. She hated him. When Sasha had politely informed Cindy that the man on stage had placed a forget-me spell on her and worse, he was Sasha's brother, Cindy couldn't believe her luck. All this time in the human realm and her senses had been tricked by a simple casting spell.

"You put a forget-me spell on me. You're a bastard!" shouted Cindy, not caring if anyone heard her.

"Actually, I'm not."

"Not what?" Cindy shivered, wishing she'd worn sensible nylons or a plain business suit instead of a short red dress with bare legs. She attempted to ignore him and then glanced to the side, cursing herself immediately. Gone was the swimsuit. Now he wore faded blue jeans, a white shirt that clung to his muscled torso and a black leather jacket, and of course the requisite Zorro mask. He looked so magically sexy a hum of energy vibrated around him, causing her nipples to pucker with need and a slow, steady pulse to burn in her pussy.

"I'm not a bastard. I'm your coworker."

He grabbed her arm when she would have stumbled with his truthful declaration.

"Coworker? No you're not." She gasped the words in complete shock and disbelief.

Mesmerized, she watched him take off the mask. "Oh my god. Lance. Is it really you?"

He nodded, watching her face intently for her reaction.

"But...but..."

"But what, Cindy?"

His Darklander Graco-Roman blue eyes took in her shivering form. She knew her nipples were poking hard through the dress fabric but she wasn't about to give him the satisfaction of knowing his caressing gaze affected her.

"You never before smelled like a magical being."

He grinned. The smile, hard around the edges and secretive, didn't reach his eyes. "But I do now, right?"

Cindy instantly inhaled. His scent, that heady melting candy apple smell, wormed its way through her body. It was the most decadent thing she had smelled since leaving her world.

She nodded. Still gripping her arm, he pulled her body to his. Without thought Cindy closed her eyes, hating how much she liked the hot candy smell of him that was mixed with pure testosterone.

"Do I smell magical, Cindy?" He breathed the words into her neck. Shock rooted her to the spot. Caged nicely in his muscular arms, Cindy was seeing a side of Lance that was seductive, potent and dangerous. Gone was the mild-mannered, polite business man. The man standing before her was a true Darklander warlock, a warrior with magic coursing through his veins. The transformation was as dramatic as day and night. It left her breathless.

Wetting her lips, she boldly assessed him.

Still tempting her exposed neck with his warm breath, he said, "I love the way you smell like hot sweet cotton candy I could eat all day. That's exactly what I did to you last night, Cindy. I ate you. All of you. Fucked you. And you enjoyed it so much you begged me again and again for more, and I was only too happy to oblige."

Cindy pushed against his chest, hating the effect of his words on her body. Her panties were wet with desire and her nipples achy for the rough feel of his tongue and mouth.

"Stop that," she demanded.

He chuckled, hauling her ass with both of his large hands more intimately to his body. She felt the tight bulge in his jeans and hated how pleased she was, knowing that he too was affected by his words.

With one snap of his fingers the world tilted in on itself. Magic pulsed around her, brushing her mind with light. She squeezed her eyes shut. Groaning, she opened them only to discover it was worse than she'd imagined.

"I'm not letting you get away. It's time the real Cindy came out to play."

She wished he hadn't spoken because his magical voice stole through her body, caressing her with breezy warmth. She turned, prepared to demand he send her back but for the life of her she couldn't speak.

She knew she was standing in Lance's bedroom. His king-sized bed with the bold dark blue duvet covering it looked as inviting as sin. She inhaled, smelling that tantalizing scent of him, all sweet melting candy, which caused her blood to boil with want. There standing before her was Lance, the Darklander warlock, bare to her direct gaze. His sun-kissed body was all hard planes, with muscular arms and thighs that led to a lean torso torpedoed with muscles. He had the perfect amount of black, curly chest hair, which her fingers itched to caress. His thick, hard cock jutted out proudly, and the purple vein of his shaft strained with desire as it bucked on its own under the discernable scrutiny of her gaze. Casually he placed his hands on his hips.

"I'm going to fuck you, Cindy, and this time you're going to remember who's thrusting his cock into that sheath of yours. It's me. Lance Papadopoulos. That's Pa-pa-do-pou-los. And I'm not your average human warlock. I'm a Darklander Graco-Roman warlock and proud of it."

He enunciated his last name through clenched teeth. It dawned on Cindy that he didn't know she was from their realm.

Graco-Roman. A Darklander Papadopoulos. The reality of the situation Cindy found herself in caused her to lean toward the bed, which was directly to her right.

"I can't. We can't."

An evil chuckle followed her pitiful declaration. "We did and will." He sauntered forward, his shaft bouncing along with his confident macho stride.

The only way Cindy could escape was with the use of magic, which would mean she'd have wielded it three times within the last forty-eight hours. The first time, she remembered was when she'd spelled Lance away from her house the night he'd shown up, causing her to realize he was a magical being. The second time she had inadvertently used magic to shut up Sasha who had been about to blab to her human friends that Cindy was a witch. The consequences of her actions would not go unnoticed, but what choice did she have?

A Papadopoulos and Stephanopoulos together. The shock of it would reverberate louder than a dozen broomsticks exploding through the Darklander realm. *This can't be. We can't be.*

"Make haste, Cindy. Take chase, Cindy. Away, away before he says nay." The power of her sing-song spell cascaded in a mad rush through her cells, flashing her away from Lance's home. It didn't bode well that her last glance at Lance had been of him smiling a smug warlock-smile with his hand fisted around the base of his cock for show. Not good at all.

The minute Cindy materialized in her house she knew she wasn't alone. The pungent odor of her mother, reminding her of black licorice, made her wrinkle her nose in distaste. For a moment she thought about spelling herself back to Lance, wondering which was the lesser of the two evils.

Her mother's casting blue eyes focused in glee upon Cindy and instantly she knew she'd made the wrong choice.

A chuckle quickly descended upon the room.

"What is that?" Her mother's sharp black eyebrows creased with annoyance. Never fear, just annoyance.

"That's a warlock."

Cindy watched her mother cast a disbelieving eye around her small townhouse, probably taking note she hadn't brought her familiar and hadn't placed any protective sugar around the openings to her dwelling. She was for all intents and purposes a sitting witch.

"Where is your familiar?" barked her mother.

"I gave it away." Cindy strolled past her mother and headed into the kitchen. Usually she went for alcohol like humans, but not now. Tonight she went straight to her stash of flavored jellybeans. When in a desperate situation the best thing to soothe her frayed nerves was colorful, tasty sugar. The momentary high she hoped to achieve by cramming a handful of jellybeans into her mouth might give her enough strength to deal with what she knew would come next—her mother meeting Lance, a Papadopoulos warlock.

"Cindy Stephanopoulos, Darklander witches don't give their familiars away. Where is she?"

"Where is who?"

Lance's baritone voice jarred her mother. For a moment Cindy almost felt sorry for her mother, but that emotion quickly dissipated the second she noticed her mother using her hands to cast a deadly spell directly at Lance.

"Stop it!" shouted Cindy, placing herself in the middle of the two powerful beings who were eyeing each other in total disbelief.

"Why is a Stephanopoulos witch in your house?"

"What is a Papadopoulos warlock doing coming into your dwelling?"

Cindy looked from one to the other, wondering who to answer first. Turning to her mother, she said pointedly, "Mother, you must promise me you will not kill him or spell him into anything else. Lance, the same for you. No killing, no maiming and no casting spells."

Placing her hands on her hips in one of her practiced business poses, she held her breath and waited. Her mother gave a curt nod, her eyes never leaving Lance's while Lance mumbled a yes. Satisfied she'd established some preliminary ground rules, Cindy marched back into the kitchen to grab her stash of candy and then ushered both of them to take a seat. Stuffing her mouth with jellybeans, she chewed fast and then made proper introductions.

Lance saw red. Cindy was not only a witch, but she was a Darklander Stephanopoulos witch. His night went from bad to cursedly horrible with the realization of what he'd gotten himself into.

Cindy looked nervous. She had eaten half a jar of jellybeans to help prep her for this encounter, but it didn't seem to be boosting her confidence. Lance thought that was strange. Cindy was always so sure of herself, utterly confident, bossy and smart. Seeing her act this way was a blow.

"So he's a coworker. Isn't that convenient?"

Lance did not like Cindy's mother, Sybil's, tone of voice. "We're much more than coworkers, aren't we, Cindy?" Really, what was coming over him? Why he felt the need to force the issue knowing it would be wiser, and in all probability healthier, for him if he kept his mouth shut, mystified him.

Sybil raised her hand.

"Mother, you promised."

Lance glanced at Sybil's well-manicured hands, noting every finger was adorned with expensive jeweled rings. *So she casts spells with her hands. That's a good thing to know.*

"What is this Papadopoulos warlock saying, Cindy?"

Lance watched Cindy's face turn bright pink. Her eyes darted to his. He gave a sexy grin and winked at her. She tisked and turned her attention back to her mother.

Popping two more red jellybeans in her mouth, she said, "Nothing. We're *just* coworkers."

He didn't miss her emphasis on the just. "Liar, liar pants on fire."

"Stop that."

"Daughter of mine, you will tell me the truth. What have you been doing with this warlock?"

Normally Cindy would tilt her chin up in defiance, square her shoulders and marshal her quick wit with a saucy retort. That's exactly what she always did when they worked together. Instead she simply shook her head. *Pitiful.*

However, the warlock side of Lance was in a foul mood. "We've been screwing around."

"Screwing around?" Sybil's voice wavered and squeaked.

Finally he'd unhinged the mighty straitlaced Stephanopoulos witch. A moment of utter delight, like that which he felt when he cut his opponent first, caused him to preen. Then he took in Cindy's horrified expression and the dagger-like stare she cast his way. Regret washed away his euphoric champion feeling. That feeling only lasted for a few seconds when he recalled exactly what the Stephanopoulos witches had done to his family for generations.

"Fucking to be precise." *Might as well go all the way with this...crude warlock that I am.*

Sybil rose in one fluid movement out of her seat. "That's impossible. A Stephanopoulos witch cannot have sex with a Papadopoulos warlock."

Something wasn't right. Sybil wasn't offended with the notion of her daughter having sex— it was the concept that they could actually do it.

"It's not possible. The curse—"

Lance stood up, using his height to tower over Sybil. "What about the curse?" He watched her fist her hands together and immediately prepared his body for a zap. Instead she took a breath and relaxed her threatening pose.

"Yes, Mother, what about the curse?" asked Cindy, who had stood up the exact moment her mother had. *Not a lot of trust there.*

"You do know that it was a Stephanopoulos witch who cast a spell on all the Papadopoulos warlocks."

Lance and Cindy nodded.

"He did deserve the punishment."

"Mother, really. That's ancient history. You can't just go cursing an entire family because one warlock screwed around."

"Cindy, you watch your language," snapped Sybil.

"Yes, Cindy, do watch that language," teased Lance. That he could flirt with her when so much was at stake rattled his warlock senses.

"Actually when the rest of the Stephanopoulos witches found out the true extent of the curse we were able to change it a bit."

"Change it? How?" asked Lance.

"A bit? Explain." Cindy crossed her arms in a pose Lance was familiar with. It pleased him to note she didn't look nearly as nervous now. *The sugar high must finally be working.*

"You only have your powers at night, right?" asked Sybil.

Lance nodded.

"Originally, she took away all the Papadopoulos powers, but by uniting our magical abilities we were able to overrule her on that."

"Well, that's just great for me." Lance's voice was filled with hateful sarcasm.

"What else?" asked Cindy.

Sybil turned her pale blue eyes toward her daughter, causing Cindy to shiver. "I'm not going to like this, am I?" asked Cindy.

"Not one bit," replied her mother.

Feeling totally out of the loop, Lance asked the obvious. "Like what?"

"We were able to make one other amendment to the curse. To stop the curse from continuing for all generations, we added a love spell to it."

Lance frowned. "Love spell?"

"Oh no," said Cindy, plopping back onto the sofa.

"Oh yes. It went something like this. With a kiss true, love will rule, binding two together, breaking what was cursed. But play me a fool, break my heart true then both the Papadopoulos and Stephanopoulos will be through."

It took Lance a good two minutes to digest the true meaning of the complicated spell. When he did his eyes widened in utter disbelief. "Wait a sec, are you saying that because Cindy and I are able to..." He gulped. No longer going for the crude approach, he amended his tirade. "Are you implying because we can get it on together we love each other?"

A smug smile and nod from Sybil was his answer.

"That can't be," said ever-practical Cindy.

"She's right, that's just silly. Magical nonsense." Lance ignored his heart, which had accelerated with the notion he might be in love with Cindy. *Maybe lust, but certainly not love.*

"Touch me," demanded Sybil.

A dumbfounded look creased Lance's face. "What?"

"Just do it."

Fine, whatever. Lance reached out to touch her hand. The instant his finger touched her flesh he got knocked on his ass by a powerful spell.

Cindy stood up. "I said no spells!"

"I didn't spell him, the curse did. Only a Stephanopoulos and Papadopoulos who are meant to be are able to touch, or as you so delicately placed it, *get it on.*"

Lance shook off his fall and stood up. The knowledge Sybil could be right burned into him. The warlock he had become grinned in earnest. "So, just to clarify things...Cindy is mine to do what I will with."

Her mother nodded.

"No I am not. I'm my own person. And I don't want to be with him."

"You do, you just won't admit it because you've always been too stubborn for your own good. Listen well, daughter of mine. This is a complicated spell. Your actions will affect both our previous and our future generations. And you, Lance—this is your one chance the magic of the universe has thrown your way to prove that a Darklander Papadopoulos warlock is true to his heart and word. Ruin it and we both shall suffer. Now I must be off. I need to discuss this with the Witches' Coven."

Lance watched Cindy's eyes dart from him to her mother.

"So I can stay on Earth?" she asked.

Her mother crossed her arms over her chest. "For now, but take my warning to heart. Make me proud...for once." Then with a curt nod Sybil flashed herself away.

Alone and together at last and with the words of the love spell still ringing in his warlock head, Lance smiled. Advancing, he took the slightly shocked Cindy into his arms, bringing her body up close and personal to his.

"Where did you think you were going?"

"Back to the Darklander world to join the Graco-Roman Witches' Coven. That had been the original deal when I said I disowned my magical powers."

"Why would you want to do that?" Lance couldn't fathom wanting to give up magic. It didn't make sense.

"I wanted to be independent, make my own way on my own merits."

Now *that* he understood. But a little magic never hurt anyone. "So you gave up magic."

She nodded. "Yes. But if I broke the bargain and used magic three times within one moon cycle I would be a servant to the Witches' Coven for life. And thanks to you, that's exactly what has happened." She attempted to push out of his hold.

Lance was having none of that. He had always admired her inner fire but now with her magical abilities she truly was like no other. His lips descended on hers without question.

It was time for action. He plundered her lush lips, not caring that he acted harsh. She yielded slightly, a small opening and he took it. Thrusting his tongue into her warm mouth, he used his hand to angle her head to his liking. A small moan escaped her. He grinned while kissing her. One hand snaked down to cup her ass, leveraging her up more so she could feel his erection, straining with need against his jeans zipper.

Cindy tilted her head back, her light blue eyes locked with his. "You don't really believe all that nonsense about true love, do you?"

He chuckled. "Not one bit. But I do believe in kissing true and just to show you how deadly serious I am..." Lance snapped his fingers, magically transporting them to her bed, naked.

She gave a small squeak of alarm. He hugged her closer, letting his cock rub into her silky smooth belly.

"You do know that you can use your magic now, right?"

A mischievous glint flashed in her eyes. "That's right. Tie you up, tie you down, let's make love with sound."

Lance laughed, giving a hard yank to the leather restraints he found himself in within seconds. He lay spread-eagle on the bed, tied to the four bedposts with soft romantic music playing in the background. He couldn't have been happier.

"I think I'm going to thoroughly enjoy the magical side of you, Cindy."

"I certainly hope so," she murmured, her tongue licking its way down his flexing abdomen.

She kissed his bellybutton and then went lower to cup his testicles in one hand while bypassing his aching cock to lick his balls. Lance lowered his head, his teeth gnashing together as the magical surge of her caresses skirted across his body. While she licked his balls and then slowly teased the wide column of his shaft, still not taking the head into that sweet hot mouth of hers, she used one hand to pebble his nipples into achy points. Bursting and ready to beg for her to take him into her mouth, she straddled his thighs and with a feather-stroke, licked the slit at the head of his cock, her tongue tasting his cum. Lance couldn't help himself. He bucked his hips up to her and yanked hard on his bonds in a desperate silent plea.

"Is there something you'd like?" Her voice was full of magic, stroking every cell in his body with lust. Cindy rubbed her wet pussy on his thigh, ensuring he understood she too was ready, crazed with the need to fuck senseless all night.

"My cock, your mouth. Now," groaned Lance.

"My pleasure."

The hot tease of her breath up and around the base and column of his shaft caused more pre-cum to seep from the slit. This time she took the entire head into her mouth. Lance groaned, the sound tearing from him with the intensity of her slick, hot mouth. She sucked, licked and pumped him for all he was worth. He answered her desire by bucking his hips up to meet her mouth.

"Come inside my mouth." Her erotic words, taking control of the situation, were the only encouragement Lance needed. He came in a hot jet, his cum sliding down Cindy's throat. She sucked and licked him clean, taking the time to caress his semi-hard cock.

Lance looked down at her lovely blonde hair strewn around her naked body and a raw emotion he had never experienced before surfaced. The notion that he could love this witch rocked his universe.

"You're amazing," he said. A second later he snapped his fingers and their roles were reversed.

"I like your line of thinking," teased Cindy, lying spread-eagle on the bed with her limbs tied to the bedposts as if she were his prisoner. The warlock he was thoroughly loved the sight.

Honing in on her wet cunt, he gave her pussy a rough lick. Lance realized in earnest as the magical scent of her sex slammed into his subconscious that Cindy really had cast a spell on him. He hoped he was warlock enough to break it.

Chapter Five

Lance felt completely exasperated. The last two days felt as if he'd once again undergone the required warlock training before becoming a full-fledged magical being with honors. The honors part he'd received only after making his first kill. The urge to kill someone rippled through him. Sometimes it felt as if he wanted to murder Cindy because she drove him insane with lust. Lance knew it was much more than the great, very physical, sex they shared that had him truly tied in knots. The knowledge he could break the damn curse that had been leveled at his family for generations fueled every other waking thought.

The diner door closed abruptly, breaking into his thoughts. Lance glanced up and watched Mitch slide into the seat opposite Hank. Both men looked as if they'd been through the wringer. Then it dawned on Lance that Mitch had just sauntered in from the outside and the sun hadn't set.

"You okay?" Lance turned his eyes to his vampire buddy. Sunset was in two and a half hours and then he'd have all his warlock magic, but until then he was basically human—thanks to that curse.

"Yeah. I think. I'm feeling slightly off," said Mitch.

Lance grinned, feeling slightly off himself. Discussing Mitch's problems made him feel better about his own.

"Why don't you tell us why you're so happy, Lance?" asked Mitch, taking his fork in his hand so he could start pushing the food around on his plate.

Lance wished he had another cup of coffee but that would make it his sixth in two hours. Instead he popped two jellybeans he'd smuggled out of Cindy's house into his mouth. "Oh I'm all peachy. I'm just grand. Did I mention that I found out how to break my family's curse?"

His buddies stopped joking in the small confines of the corner booth and actually sat up straighter to listen.

"No shit. Spill," demanded Mitch.

"Yup, all it takes is true love."

They chuckled teasingly at him.

"Let me guess, true love is none other than your coworker," said Hank.

Lance nodded.

"Why is that bad?" asked Mitch.

Lance sat back in his booth and crossed his arms over his chest. "She's a Darklander Stephanopoulos witch."

"You are kidding, right?" asked Hank.

"Nope. Cindy is actually Cindy Stephanopoulos Frost and get this, guys, her mother is a member of the Graco-Roman Coven and she'd love to turn me into a toad and then throw me into her cauldron. Let me tell you, she wasn't one bit happy with this turn of events."

"How did Cindy take it?" asked Mitch.

"She laughed it off, but then again she would. It's not as if her family were cursed or anything like that. Mind you, if what her mother said is true then both our families will cease to exist if we mess this up."

"By the way, I never understood that curse of yours. Why is it that your sister isn't affected?" asked Mitch, reaching to put his black shades on.

Lance cast an evil glance his way. "It's a male curse. Only we warlocks were blessed with being cursed. I've got to run. See you tonight."

Hank stood up. "Those women did something to us and I personally think they fucked us over royally. I've got to go to work. Are you guys still strutting your stuff tonight?"

"If we don't, my sister will turn us all into lizards," muttered Lance.

"I thought she'd turn us into toads," said Mitch.

"Nah, she likes lizards more than toads. She enjoys catching them to see their tails fall off," said Lance.

Mitch stood up, pushing the food on his plate far away from him. "That's sick. Personally, I think we should boycott it."

Lance tossed a twenty-dollar bill onto the table. "You boycott it and see how my sister makes you feel. If you think your life is fucked up now, trust me, you don't want to mess with one seriously pissed-off witch."

"I really don't want to go," mumbled Mitch.

"I wouldn't worry about it. The gals probably won't show up. After all, I did keep Nora up all night," said Hank.

"Yeah, when I left this morning, Cindy was still asleep. Poor witch. I think after last night she'll probably call in sick and spend the entire day in bed."

"Don't you and she work for the same company?"

"Yeah, well, I called in sick today, also," said Lance sheepishly.

"Well then, man, seems as if she wore you out," teased Hank.

"We should have said no to your sister from the beginning," stated Mitch, stepping through the diner door and into the settling dusk.

"You try saying no to my sister, good luck with that one. See you later. Mitch, take care."

Lance watched his buddy stroll casually away, pleased to note he wasn't burning up from the sunlight streaking through the darkening clouds. Forty-five minutes more and Lance would be in full warlock mode. As he walked back to his apartment he contemplated all that had transpired in the past forty-eight hours. Finally after years of searching for a cure to his family's curse he was going to exact his revenge on the Stephanopoulos witches. He had a duty to uphold.

They deserve whatever they get. A twinge of fear spiraled through him. If what Cindy's mother said was true then by exacting his revenge on the Stephanopoulos witches he could wipe out his own Papadopoulos history.

She's probably lying. All Stephanopoulos witches lie. But not Cindy. She's different. She's more Frost than one of those Darklander crones. Lance knew Cindy wouldn't like him comparing her with her mother but really, they were as different as night and day.

* * * * *

Cindy swore from the moment she walked into the auction for the final night of the fundraiser that all she could smell was sticky hot melting candy. It left her feeling hungry and achy for Lance and that wasn't good.

And things weren't progressing like she thought they would. The only reason she'd shown up for the event was because all three of them had agreed to go every night. And now her friends were bailing on her.

"Hey, where did my friends go?" asked Cindy, the minute Sasha strode toward her table. The smell of melting chocolate wafted around Sasha, making it hard for Cindy to concentrate.

Night three of the charity auction was totally out of this world, thought Cindy. First her friend Nora left in a huff and then Tina strolled up onstage to take the place of the woman Mitch had draped under his arm.

"It's a wild night, Cindy, let it all go," said Sasha cryptically.

Cindy feigned a smile. "Is that supposed to make sense, Sasha?"

"You can't please everyone, but you should please yourself."

"Okay, that didn't even rhyme," huffed Cindy, popping more candies into her mouth.

Sasha leaned on Cindy's table, her pink witch's hat almost tilting off her head. "Enjoy. My brother's a good warlock and you're a good..."

"Don't even say it," said Cindy. "I need a refill." She handed the empty jellybean bowl to Sasha.

"You can do that yourself. Trust in your own magic." Those were Sasha's parting words. A gasp from the crowd informed Cindy that another show had started. The stage lights were back on and why did it not surprise her that Lance was the one strutting his stuff? However, this was a Lance she didn't know. Gone was his traditional tailored business suit. This Lance commanded the crowd to watch him—her magical-sexy Darklander warlock who made her instantly think of hard, sticky lollypops. *Oh yeah, I'd like to lick something all right and it's hard, sticky and can make my warlock groan for more.* Inwardly, Cindy giggled at her racy thoughts. *Wait a sec, he's not my warlock. I did not think that. I most certainly did not. Oh my, I'm having an argument with myself and that's not good.*

Then all of Cindy's thoughts scattered.

Lance wore the traditional warlock attire and was met with a round of giggles from the crowd. The only one not giggling was Cindy. *Magically hot.* That description aptly fitted Lance, who ignored the chuckles. The minute he tore off the long dark velvet robe no woman laughed. His back rippled with muscles as he expertly slashed the air with the long saber in his hand. The skin-tight black pantaloons he wore showcased more of his assets than she liked. He flung the sword up high and caught it on bended knee with one hand. The sword came to rest half an inch from his crotch. Awed by his warrior display, the women oohed for more.

Cindy, however, did not want more. She didn't think her heart or body could stand watching him attempt to neatly slice and dice his body parts. A red haze of smoke filled the stage and startled gasps tore through the crowd.

"I am your knight. I am your warrior. I am yours." Lance's voice was pure red wine, tempting every woman in the room. He made the words sound intimate but Cindy knew he'd meant them for her. Inwardly, she preened while fishing around for more jellybeans. Realizing she had eaten all her own personal stash and that the bowl on the table was still empty left her edgy.

"Warlock, save me."

The husky, seductive voice came from the stage. Cindy could not believe her eyes. *What is this?* There on the stage, scantily clad, was a beautiful witch. She had long flaming orange-hued hair, and big breasts filled out the Darklander Zirta-like outfit she'd taken the time to put on. *Give me a break.* The outfit looked about two sizes too small as the tight, black bustier lifted her breasts up for everyone to see.

"Hey, who's she?" asked someone from the crowd.

Yeah, that's right, who's she?

"She's my damsel in distress and I will save her from this menace."

Cindy truly wished Lance wouldn't speak. It was night and every cell within his body was overflowing with magic. The rumble of his voice was bespelled to fulfill every woman's fantasy. For her that meant it left her feeling as if she'd been soaking in a refreshing peppermint bath...tingling her with want, desire and the mad impulse to put an end to his shenanigans on stage. *Wait a sec, aren't I his damsel in distress?*

"Save me, warlock. I will spell you a gift."

Shut up! Cindy was getting totally pissed with the other woman's lovey-dovey-witchy voice. The urge to bolt, flee the crowd or zap the other witch into a toad caused Cindy to crack a smile. She laced her fingers together in a prayer-like pose and channeled her thoughts into her normal business approach.

I will not give in to the urge to do a casting. I will not be tempted by magic. Reciting her internal prayer allowed her to gather her strength. She desperately needed that when a menacing roar startled everyone in the crowd. A green puff of smoke smelling like a huge pile of manure quickly hit her nose. Cindy knew that smell. Every witch knew the pungent odor of the drákon. It was something all Darklander witches were taught to avoid at all costs.

No way. That's impossible. It couldn't be a drákon. Not a real drákon. That's just insane.

Sasha ran through the crowd. Openly, she weaved her wand here and there, casting what looked like safe shields around the patrons, who all looked shell-shocked. And who wouldn't? There onstage in its spectacular battle armor was what looked like a real drákon. A flash of fire spewed forth from his mouth. The heat of it caused Cindy's fantasy to explode.

Standing up, she bellowed out to Sasha, "Hey, is that a real drákon?"

All Lance's sister could do was nod as she ducked a fiery blast the beast directed at her.

"Save me, warlock. Save me," whined the pathetic witch now secured to a beam.

Where did that beam come from? Really, this fantasy come to life has a mind of its own. Cindy felt completely out of sorts.

Lance however did not look one bit out of his element. He sported a wide, sexy grin. His blue eyes danced with devilment and delight, clearly savoring the challenge of saving the witch-damsel while destroying the drákon. Part of Cindy actually rooted for the drákon to make a meal out of the whiny witch. However, her tactic changed the second the drákon zoned in on her.

Spellbound, she watched as the large, eight-foot reptilian creature made a lumbering move in her direction. Drákon were slow, but with their unique body armor that had flashy red rubies, green emeralds and shiny diamonds encrusted all over it, and with their ability to spew forth fire, they were truly a force to be reckoned with. Plus their love of eating witches was notorious.

"Don't run, Cindy."

Lance's words didn't make any sense. Every instinct within her said to flee the scene.

"Hey, stinky-beast, come and get me."

Lance waved his arm and sword madly around in an attempt to get the beast to zone in on him. Cindy's heart warmed. *Now that's my warlock-warrior.*

Sasha worked her way over to where Cindy stood. "I did not call forth that damn creature."

"What?" Cindy had clearly thought that's exactly what Sasha had done.

"That bitch-witch up on stage did this. I told her she couldn't participate because I don't like her and she pulls a stunt like this. To top it off, Lance thinks he's invincible. He thinks this is part of the show, because she put a mind-spell on him. I am *so* going to kill her."

Cindy totally echoed Sasha's rant.

"And I can't help him."

"What do you mean?" asked Cindy. "You're a witch. Of course you can help him."

"Sadly no. She made sure I couldn't. She cast a warding on all family members. Oh my, this isn't good. I'm going to have to zap all these humans out of here. Will you help?"

Numbly, Cindy nodded.

"Human, humans, away, away, back to your homes you will stay," chanted Cindy.

"Thank you. While you did that I cast a spell on them to ensure they won't remember a thing."

In the midst of the chaos now taking place on the stage, Sasha managed to smile. A feeling of belonging, of finally coming home, crashed into Cindy. "You're welcome," she mumbled. Cindy stole a glance to the stage area. Things did not look good for Lance. "Hey, why isn't he using his magic?"

"I'm sure that bitch-witch cast a spell on him too. I am so going to enjoy turning her into a toad."

"I thought you'd turn her into a lizard."

"I have my standards. I like lizards. I do not like toads. Plus, if I cast her into a toad I get to enjoy catching her and watching her hop up and down."

Cindy's eyes widened. "That's sick."

56 Be My Warlock Tonight

"I know. You do realize that you're going to have to save him."

"Me?" squeaked Cindy, taking a step back, while Sasha ducked to avoid a blast the drákon spewed their way.

"You're not officially family *yet*. Save him. I'm going to call for reinforcements because that bitch of a witch never plays fair as you can see. See what I mean? She's always lusted after Lance, and she's taking great delight that she's ruined my finale."

Cindy heard "lusted after Lance" and any trace of a friendly thought she might have had toward the witch onstage exploded like a wild broomstick.

"Lusted? What exactly do you mean?"

Clarification, that's exactly what Cindy wanted. When faced with a business problem always get all the facts. If she didn't like them, so be it.

"Okay, they had a brief history but it really was nothing."

Cindy wasn't sure she digested what Sasha said because her body flushed hot with a mad zap of magic.

"Be still, be still, you casting evil will. Bind and gag you, I contain you." The chant soared through the room and then whammo, eerie silence filled the space.

"Thank you," mouthed Sasha, making her way up to the stage where the bitch-witch was currently gagged and bound to the post, all thanks to Cindy's spell. The drákon was frozen in place and Lance clutched his head in agony.

"What happened?" His voice, still laced with magical charm, caused Cindy's heart to accelerate and her nipples to strain toward him.

He took one look at her and zapped himself beside her. Cindy knew she shouldn't allow him to pull her to his hot, sleek body, but the magical part of her ached to do so. She leaned into him, inhaling that hot candy scent. *Wait a sec, what am I doing?*

As if he knew her business mind had kicked into high gear, Lance wrapped his steel arms around her and with one snap of his fingers she found herself back in his bed, naked. As always the mad rush of the use of magic that fueled her cells through time and space left her feeling shaky with need. Slowly she opened her eyes.

There on his knees was her warlock. His cock jutted out its own welcome as it throbbed at her. Lance grinned, looking mighty pleased with himself. *And why shouldn't he be?* He got what he wanted. Cindy didn't want to finish that sentence because she knew after all that had happened in the past few days she got what she wanted—her magical, Darklander warlock all to herself, and that knowledge truly damned her.

Chapter Six

"Suck it."

Her warlock was once again issuing orders. Cindy smiled. This was one order she desperately wanted to obey. Turning her head, she made sure Lance watched her tongue wet her lips. His eyes half closed with desire. "Put it in my mouth," she boldly teased.

He didn't hesitate. Her tongue swirled around his cock, loving the feel of the firm column as it slid into her mouth to her gag reflex. With willpower she relaxed to allow him to push it into her throat. Pre-cum seeped out of him, the salty flavor of Lance an erotic recipe all on its own. Her hand wrapped around his base, allowing her to pump him as her mouth worked him with business-like detail.

His head fell back with pleasure. Cindy turned to her side, enabling her to take more of his shaft into her mouth. With her other hand she snaked it up to his nipples, pinching hard. His balls bounced into her face. She repeated her action with his other nipple until both were tight, pebbled nubs.

His caressing magic slid around her body, making her tingle in all the right places. While she was intent on ensuring he had pleasure, Lance also wanted to make sure he pleased her. She smiled around his cock, taking the time to lick the thick vein that pulsed for release.

Lance used a magical charm to make it feel as if his hands were skimming all over her body. The effect was twofold—highly erotic but a subtle reminder he was a magical being to the core. She wanted to hate him because he easily embraced the magic that lived within him without thought. In fact he truly loved it. *Maybe if I were cursed and could only wield magic at night I'd wish for it too.* The morose thought flashed like a neon sign inside of Cindy.

Lance pushed his cock deeper, willing her to pay attention to him. Blinking up at him, she noticed his sure grin. Taking the time to memorize every nuance of his shaft and testicles, she rose to her knees, ensuring he came along for the ride. A rugged groan slipped from his lips. Fisting her hand around the base of his cock, she pumped him hard, causing his six-pack abdomen to flex. His breathing grew shallow, his eyes closed and his hands fisted as he sought control.

This was her time. Lance attempted to edge off the bed, yanking her blonde hair. She shook her head, keeping his cock wedged between her teeth and subtle tongue. Tenderly her tongue swirled around his wide column, and she moaned as the salty flavor of him settled into her.

"Cindy, I'm going to come if you keep that up."

Lance's admission was all she needed. With a sexy witch smile full of magical charm Cindy decided to go for it. Chanting the magical charm in her head, she did as he had—making it feel as if her hands were all over his body. He muffled a curse and bucked his hips up, causing her to momentarily gag as the fullness of his cock got crammed down her throat. She'd pushed him past the point of no return. The mantle of control Lance wore tore free and she welcomed it. His hips pumped into her mouth and she opened wider, allowing him to thrust as deep as he could. Her hands moved to his heavy sac, grasping it with one hand while moving a delicate finger to play with the crack of his ass.

He stilled, breathing deep, trying once again to assert control. She didn't want that. Without thought to the consequences, Cindy let a finger wedge deep into the tight hole of his ass. He gave one last thrust—grasping her head to ensure she didn't escape. Then he came, the hot spurt of his seed raining down into her mouth, filling her. She gulped, tasting his magical essence, loving the salty and sweet flavor of him. Licking him clean, she flopped onto her back.

"You like?"

Lance gave her a long, thorough hot look that set Cindy's body and mind on fire. There was something telling, something that had changed because she'd dared take control. A shiver of desire swamped her magical senses.

She thought his kiss would be brutal. It was the exact opposite. Featherlight, he took her slightly swollen bottom lip into his mouth, tasting his own passion. She yielded, opening her mouth to his loving lips. And it was loving. It wasn't a taking or a thank you. No, in her heart Cindy sensed the difference.

The melding of their combined magical energy coalesced into one entity with the power of his kiss. Her heart went straight into overdrive with the realization this was beyond her control. This was pure, unbridled universal-soul power, eating her alive with passion. She had no control over her emotions and realized no amount of business sense would save her from falling magically in love with Lance.

Lance wanted the feel of his body on top of Cindy's. He wanted her breasts pushing into his chest, he needed the feel of his still-hard cock against her slick cunt and he had to have those blue eyes that looked so sexy with want and filled with magic watching him as he took her.

His heart skipped a beat as he looked at the lovely Darklander witch lying beneath him. Her long, cascading blonde hair spilled with a life of its own around his pillows. Her hot, melting candy scent reminded him of a bouquet of fresh flowers with a hint of cinnamon as it filled his bedroom. He couldn't have been happier. Her body hummed with magic. Now that she'd given in to her magical essence, varying shades of yellow colors surrounded her with brilliance. It was like looking at a Goddess come to life—warrior and lover sinfully combined into the best magical beauty of all time.

"I love you."

Lance had no idea where the words came from. Cindy's eyes popped open, the effect showcasing the surprise and fear his words had evoked.

"No, you do not. You're just saying that because of the curse."

Her easy answer didn't sit well with him. He leaned back, crouching, still needing to be seated between the vee of her thighs, wanting to see the slick dew of her pussy that screamed she was ready for the taking. He liked that. Cindy wasn't shy, didn't cower in the bedroom pretending she didn't enjoy what they were doing. She was the type of woman, type of witch who relished all the ways they could fuck. A hot, fast-pounding fuck or a slow, tender loving one suited her fine. Depending on her mood she could be just as dirty, just as ferocious or inventive as him. Lance ran his hands through his tousled hair.

It wasn't like him to casually throw out meaningless words. That wasn't the warlock he was or the man he could be. He hadn't thought about the impact of his words but he realized he meant them.

"The curse has nothing to do with it and you know it."

She attempted to prop herself up onto her elbows. He leaned over her, keeping her in her prone position.

"The curse has everything to do with it."

She looked angry and scared. Lance wished he was angry but he wasn't. He no longer quested for revenge on the Stephanopoulos witches—it no longer mattered. The only thing important to him was Cindy. He wanted her. Now and always and it was about time he became the Darklander warlock he was and fully made her his.

In his heart Lance knew he should ask permission but he was afraid she'd rebuff him.

"You pick. Do you want me to fuck you or love you?"

She didn't hesitate. "Fuck me."

Her clipped answer was all bravado and he knew it. "Turn over, on your knees now."

Oh he was going to take her, just not how she expected. Cindy gave him a coy look, following his instructions, flashing her ass high, letting him know she was attempting to take control.

He pushed her face into his pillow and leaned all his weight onto her. She groaned. He knew exactly how she felt. The heat of their bodies was like the Darklander outer realm, full of hot magic. Lance's hands circled her waist, toying with her belly as he made his way to her heaving breasts. He tweaked first one nipple and then the other. Cindy's head thrashed around on the pillow as she gave in to the passion surging through her body. Widening her stance, Lance took his cock in hand, sliding it over her wet cunt. She whimpered. He was tempted to plunge it into her pussy, pounding her with his lust, but she'd wanted to fuck so he was going to do it his way.

Lance moved his cock to the crack of her ass, letting his pre-cum slide along the tight crease. She tensed for a moment and then relaxed. He pushed his shaft against her tight hole, watching her body's reaction.

"Relax," he said, wedging it a fraction of an inch inside her ass.

"What are you doing?" A cautionary note crept into her voice but it wasn't fear. That pleased him.

"Fucking you...like you asked. Trust me, you'll enjoy it."

Slowly and with care Lance used a bit of magic to lube Cindy's virgin hole. Then he played with her sensitive area until she relaxed and then pushed a finger into her. She whimpered with newfound desire.

"You okay?" asked Lance.

Cindy turned her head to look at him. "So far I'm loving it."

Without further ado, Lance moved his body up over hers. With magic he lubed his cock again and grinned at the cool tingly feeling the lotion induced on his engorged penis. Then he pushed his cock all the way into her hole. She stilled. He gave her a minute to adjust to his size and then slowly withdrew.

"More," she said, panting.

Grinning, he pumped his cock back inside, this time snaking a hand around to her front to play with her wet pussy. His fingers easily found her pebbled nub and he tweaked it hard.

Cindy leveraged her ass to meet him. The sensation of him filling her ass was something she'd never thought she would enjoy, but Lance had used his magic to read her mind and it pleased him knowing he was able to awaken a new pleasure spot on her body. Lance kept up his play with her nub. She bounded back on her knees to meet his thrusts while he kept plunging his cock into her ass until the urge to come once again took hold of him. Gripping her hips, he came long and hard inside her.

Ensuring she followed suit, he patted her hard achy clit, sending her into an orgasm that had her inner muscles clenching around him in pleasure.

Withdrawing slowly, he flashed a warm basin of water and towel to the side of his bed. Lance lovingly used the warm wash cloth to clean Cindy and himself. Then he flashed them both to his warm Jacuzzi.

Cindy used magic to bind her hair up off her shoulders, ensuring it didn't get soaked. Soft, light gold tendrils slid down both sides of her face, evoking a girlish pose. Usually Cindy was all polished business but no longer. She seemed softer, more refined and he loved her all the more for it.

"You said you were going to fuck me."

"Did I?" Lance moved toward her, bridging the small gap separating them.

"You did."

It was a strange argument and Lance knew she used the harsh words in her attempt to claim he didn't love her.

"You just want me to say it again, don't you?" His teasing words caused a sad smile to flirt across her face.

"I'm not lovable?"

"Says who?" He braced his arms on either side of her body as it lay against the sides of the Jacuzzi.

"I can't do anything right. I don't even want to be a witch."

Lance chuckled. She playfully smacked him in the shoulder. He feigned affront but still smiled. Cupping her chin in his hand, Lance looked Cindy in the eyes. "Cindy, you can't change what you are. You're a Darklander witch through and through, and even if you weren't it wouldn't change how I feel about you. In fact, when I didn't know you were a witch I asked you out. Sadly though you refused me. Twice as I recall."

"I only did that—"

He silenced her protest by placing a finger on her lips. "I don't care for the reasons. The magic of the universe works in mysterious ways. If you're asking, am I disappointed in discovering you're a witch and a Darklander Stephanopoulos witch at that, I will admit at one time I would have said yes. But now..." Lance took the time to stare into her eyes, ensuring she listened to his choice of words. "Now that I know you, my answer is most definitely no. I love you...Cindy Stephanopoulos Frost. You and only you. Screw the curse. I don't care that I can only wield magic at night. So what? I want to make you happy. I want to spend the rest of my life slaying all those drákon just for you. You feel me?"

Tears pooled into Cindy's eyes. *Shit, this is not what I expected.*

She sniffled and then flashed a searing smile up at him. "Lance, I think you need to understand why I wanted to give up my magic."

He nodded, encouraging her on, not trusting himself to speak.

"I gave it up because I could never measure up to my mother. Every spell I did wasn't good enough for her. So for all my life I doubted my abilities and I grew to hate what I inherently was. I grew to hate everything about my culture, my identity and I didn't trust my own magic."

"But you're a great witch," he said, interrupting her.

"Thank you. Coming from you that means a lot. I had to escape my predestined path. I knew my mother was grooming me to join the Witches' Coven and that wasn't something I wanted. Can you imagine spending every waking moment with my mother?"

She laughed, the sound light and airy. Lance felt hope magically soar through his heart. "Honestly, nope. Your mother is scary."

"Trust me on that one, I know. She doesn't mean to be and I truly think she did have my best interests at heart but being a member of the Coven doesn't allow for a child like me. A child who never measures up to her mother."

It was a telling statement coming from Cindy. Lance couldn't have cared if she ever measured up to her mother but to think she thought herself unworthy when she was so much more than that caused his pain to morph into anger.

"If you're telling me you can't love me because of your mother, I'm going to spank you."

She giggled. "You don't really want me. You're just doing this to free your family from the curse."

Totally exasperated, Lance didn't know what to do to make her listen to the truth of his words so the warlock he was decided he'd kiss away all her self-doubt. Then it dawned on him, he did have another option.

Intimately touching his forehead to hers, he snapped his fingers, sending them both spiraling into the future. Two paths lay before them. One dark, the other filled with laughter and light.

"You choose."

"We're not allowed to do this," she said, caution edging into her voice.

"Before you pick the path you want us to walk down let's see our options. I won't tell anyone." Lance flashed them into the void of the future. He linked his fingers through hers, nudging Cindy forward. "Pick."

"I don't think I want to see it."

BE MY WARLOCK TONIGHT

"I never expected Cindy Stephanopoulos Frost to be a coward," Lance purposely taunted her, hoping it would spring her backbone back into place. She unhooked her fingers from his.

"Fine."

Lance watched her move toward the light. He followed on her heels and gulped. The scene blazed bright and caught at every one of his heart strings. There before him on a beach was Cindy, bouncing a toddler on her lap, her belly round and full with a second child. Her face beamed with hope and happiness, while she cast a gaze up at him. The adoration shining from his face was evident. Lance heard Cindy gasp.

"I look so happy. Children. I never expected to have children." A tear clogged her throat and he knew exactly how she felt.

"Now the other." Lance knew he was playing the bastard but he had to make sure she saw her choices clearly.

With hesitation slowing her stride, she backed away from the bright, hopeful scene. Slinking down the blackened corridor, she gave a weak cry. There was Cindy cloistered away in a gray, bleak room. His gut told him it had to be a room the Graco-Roman Witches' Coven had allotted to her. She was all business. A gray robe huddled around her as she scribed away.

"That's what will become of me." It was a stark contrast to the playful, light scene with him in her life. But again, the choice had to be hers.

"How do I choose? What if the choice isn't mine?"

A violent yellow flash tore them both from the void of the future. Landing on his feet was pure instinct for Lance.

"You are not allowed into the void."

Great, just great, thought Lance.

There standing majestic and proud before them, casting her usual judgment, was Sybil, Cindy's mother. Lance's body prepared for the zap of the attack he felt was seconds away.

67

"Mother, stop it. The magic of the universe works in mysterious ways. Lance came into my life and showed me that I should trust in my own magic."

"Of course you trust in your own magic, Cindy. Don't talk in riddles."

Cindy took a step toward her mother. A surge of pride took hold of Lance. This was the Cindy he had fallen in love with. Determined. Sure of herself and full of confidence.

"I love him."

"What?" Lance heard himself mutter while Sybil laughed. The sound wasn't at all what he had expected.

Sybil reached her daughter halfway, holding out her arms to offer an embrace. Cindy cautiously edged her way into her mother's hold. Slightly awkward at first but after a moment's hesitation they allowed themselves to give in.

"You've made me proud, daughter of mine, all your life but today the magic of the universe is our witness is your crowning glory. By accepting your magic you have enabled yourself to love him and together the two of you have broken the curse. The vows of binding love have already wrapped themselves around you."

Cindy stepped out of her mother's hold, clutching her arms. Lance smiled, feeling what she too felt. The universal seal of magic, accepting their binding love, encased both of them. Lance walked forward, hugging Cindy.

She tilted her head up to his, the brightness of her blue eyes shining up at him in total honesty. "I love you."

"I know." To prove it he kissed her, wanting it to last for all of time.

"I leave you now, daughter of mine, with the Coven's blessing for your choice. Let's keep that little trip to the future between family members." Sybil gave a small chuckle.

Lance knew Cindy wanted to break their kiss but he wasn't done with her yet. Clasping his arms around her, he flashed them back to his bed. Only then did he relinquish his hold.

"I should have said goodbye."

"Your mother surprised me."

"Not all Stephanopoulos witches are bad."

Lance kissed his way down Cindy's exposed neck, breathing deep that hot candy scent of hers that instantly made his cock throb. "There's nothing wrong with bad, it's all relative."

"Oh," she said, her hands caressing his back while boldly moving to his ass. "I like your line of thinking."

"Show me," instructed Lance. A second later he was flashed on to his back, his arms and legs shackled, once again, in restraints. His cock jutted up proud under Cindy's scrutiny. He watched her lick her lips and felt his abdomen constrict with pleasure.

"Oh I'll show you all right. After all I'm a Stephanopoulos witch all the way."

That was exactly what Lance had magically hoped for. Good or bad, it truly was all relative. He groaned the second her tongue latched onto his nipple, knowing as a Papadopoulos warlock he was in for a long, slow torturous night of pleasure.

* * * * *

Cindy couldn't believe all that had happened to her within the past week. After making her decision to fully embrace her magic she'd been shocked to discover Lance's buddies, who were currently dating her two best friends, were other Darklander beings—Mitch a vampire and Hank a werecat. Coming clean to her best friends about who she was felt perfect to Cindy. And the best part about all that had happened to her this week had been being named the new CEO for Xeron. That, she had earned on her own, all without her magical abilities. Smiling at her good fortune and thanking all the Darklander Gods and deities for her lover and soon-to-be husband and best friends, Cindy basked in the warmth when Lance whispered an erotic enticement into her ear, causing her to squirm with desire.

Before responding, her magical warlock whisked them away and before she could chant her own spell she found herself naked and chained to a brick wall. Gently Lance licked her earlobe as his hands snaked around to tweak her nipples.

"Were you about to complain?" he asked.

"Not in this world," she said, enjoying how he mastered their loving in true Darklander warlock fashion.

Other Books by Renee Field:

Follow her on Facebook at https://www.facebook.com/ReneeFieldRomanceAuthor

Twitter @pararomance

Email: reneefieldauthor@gmail.com

Titan Series:

Rapture, Titan series Book 1

Bliss, Titan series Book 2

Romance Siren series:

Claiming the Temptress (novella) (HQN Spice Briefs)

Claiming Poseidon's Heart (mythology romance)

Claiming A Siren's Heart (mythology romance)

A Siren's Wish (mythology romance)

What to Read After FSOG: The Gemstone Collection (WTRAFSOG Book 7)

Witch Me Good (Sexy Salem Witch Stories Book 1)

Spice Me Up (contemporary romance)

Heart of Mind (paranormal romance)

Queen of Dragons (paranormal romance)

Fairy Cursed (Highlander, Fey romance)

Darklander Lovers Series (paranormal romance):

Be My Vampire Tonight (Darklander Lovers, Book One)

Be My Werecat Tonight (Darklander Lovers, Book Two)

Be My Warlock Tonight (Darklander Lovers, Book Three)

Warriors of Maida (mythology sexy romance series):

Love Me Wild, Book One

Love Me Tender, Book Two

Love Me Strong, Book Three

Contemporary Romance:

Embrace (sweet contemporary romance novella)

Summer Heat (new adult romance)

Don't miss out!

Visit the website below and you can sign up to receive emails whenever Renee Field publishes a new book. There's no charge and no obligation.

https://books2read.com/r/B-A-HRN-BFZR

BOOKS 2 READ

Connecting independent readers to independent writers.

Did you love *Be My Warlock Tonight*? Then you should read *Be My Vampire Tonight*[1] by Renee Field!

Bidding on a masked man at an auction is all for a good cause, but what happens when he turns out to be a vampire who has the power to unleash the wild woman lying dormant inside you?

As a Darklander vampire, Mitch has spent a century living in a bleak world, but all that changes when he sees Tina. The beast living within Mitch wants to stake his claim. Mitch knows taking Tina's virginity will change her forever, but try explaining that to a woman whose passion cannot be denied.

Tina holds the key to his freedom, but Mitch will be damned forever before he turns her over as a slave for his master.

Book one in the Darklander Lovers series.

---

1. https://books2read.com/u/3RoMDG

2. https://books2read.com/u/3RoMDG

Read more at www.reneefield.com.

Also by Renee Field

A Warriors of Maida Novella
Love Me Wild
Love Me Tender
Love Me Strong
Love Me Wild

Darklander Lovers
Be My Warlock Tonight
Be My Vampire Tonight
Be My Werecat Tonight

Elemental Love
Heart of Mine

Riverton Cove series
Embrace

Titan series
Rapture
Bliss

Standalone
Claiming A Siren's Heart
Claiming Poseidon's Heart
A Siren's Wish
Fairy Cursed
Summer Heat
Queen of Dragons
Summer Heat
Electrify Me

Watch for more at www.reneefield.com.

About the Author

Renee loves to write a variety of genres. She writes for HQN Spice Briefs and also writes sensual paranormal romance, and contemporary romance as an Indie author. Field also writes nitty gritty young adult and paranormal young adult romance novels under the pen name Renee Pace. Renee calls Halifax, Nova Scotia, Canada home and loves her view of the Atlantic Ocean. She is a member of Romance Writers' of America, and her local Romance Writers of Atlantic Canada. She juggles work, four children and is a firm believer in soul-mates and the power of the sea.

Renee loves to hear from fans. She can be reached by email at reneefieldauthor@gmail.com

Read more at www.reneefield.com.

www.ingramcontent.com/pod-product-compliance
Lightning Source LLC
Chambersburg PA
CBHW020549130626
46552CB00007B/2829